# The Catastrophic Era:

## *Rome Versus Persia in the Third Century*

by Tim Donovan

PublishAmerica
Baltimore

First printing

At the specific preference of the author, PublishAmerica allowed this work to remain exactly as the author intended, verbatim, without editorial input.

ISBN: 1-4137-5490-2
PUBLISHED BY PUBLISHAMERICA, LLLP
www.publishamerica.com
Baltimore

Printed in the United States of America

# The Catastrophic Era:

*Rome Versus Persia*
*in the Third Century*

# Preface

The third century is shrouded in mystery. Particularly baffling is the period from 228-260, during which the Romans and Persians fought four major wars. Great battles took place about which we know next to nothing. There are widely divergent accounts of the death of one Roman emperor, and the capture of another. Sorting truth from fiction is not easy. Until recently most scholars never seriously tried. They tended to quickly pass over the third century, preferring to focus on the better-documented periods of Roman history. In recent years, however, the third century has received more emphasis, and a clearer picture has begun to emerge. Building upon recent scholarship, this book attempts to reconstruct exactly what happened, and why, in the great wars of that era.

# The Rise of Sassanian Persia

The Parthians were once formidable enemies of Rome. They were most successful toward the end of the Roman Republic. Parthian prowess was clearly demonstrated in 53 BCE when the legions of Crassus attempted to subdue the East. Mounted Parthian archers and cataphracts (armored cavalry) destroyed the legions at Carrhae. Twenty thousand Romans perished, including Crassus and his son, and 10,000 were captured along with the legionary standards. Pacorus, a Parthian general, followed up this victory by invading Roman territory. In 51 BCE his forces overran most of Syria. Unable to subdue Antioch by siege, however, Pacorus withdrew. Forty BCE witnessed another major success as Parthian troops under Pacorus and Labienus conquered most of Asia Minor and Syria before Roman reinforcements drove them back.

The last great achievements of Parthian arms in the first century

BCE occurred during the reign of Phraates IV. In 36 BCE a Roman army under Mark Anthony marched to Media Atropatene and besieged its capital, Phraaspa. Cavalry led by Phraates IV burned and plundered the Roman baggage train, forcing Anthony to withdraw. Parthian archers massacred the retreating enemy. Anthony made a second attempt the following year, but was again stymied by Parthian forces.

By the time of Augustus, the failure of Roman arms in the East had led to a more prudent policy. Augustus sought a peaceful settlement with Parthia. In 20 BCE negotiations resulted in the return of the Roman standards lost at Carrhae. The first emperor did not attempt to advance beyond the Euphrates.

The high Roman Empire, however, was to prove more successful and ambitious. Parthia held its own in the first century CE.[1] The second century, however, was to prove disastrous for the Asian nation.

Trajan brought the Roman Empire to its height of conquest. In 114 he annexed Armenia and Transcaucasia. The next year the "best of emperors" crossed the Euphrates. His legions captured Adiabene, Mesopotamia and the Parthian capital, Ctesiphon, along with the Parthian king and his daughter. The Romans faced revolts, but to some extent managed to restore order.

After Trajan's death in 117 his successor, Hadrian, ordered the abandonment of the eastern conquests. Hadrian apparently believed the Roman lines of communication had become excessively long. Some Roman generals considered the withdrawal order unwise and cowardly. Had the Romans decided to try to consolidate their grip on the East, Parthia might never have revived.[2]

Parthia fared better, at least initially, during its next major war with Rome. In 161 Vologases IV invaded Armenia. He replaced the Armenian ruler with Pacorus, from a royal Parthian family. The Roman governor of Cappodocia, Severianus, attempted to intervene in Armenia with one of his legions. This legion, IX Hispana, was trapped and destroyed by the Parthian general Chosrhoes at Elegeia. The Parthians then struck at Syria, in 162, routing the forces of Attidius Cornelianus, governor of the province.

The Parthian successes of 161-162 largely resulted from the ineffectiveness of Rome's eastern legions. They had grown slack in the urbanized East.[3] Over a century earlier, in the time of Nero, the Roman general Corbulo had to rectify the faults of the eastern troops. Now, in the early 160s, reinforcements from Europe, and a new disciplinarian, Avidius Cassius, restored the situation. The Parthians were driven back in 163, and in 165 Cassius defeated them in a major battle at Dura Europos.[4] By 166 Cassius had captured Seleucia and Ctesiphon and burned the palace of Vologases. The Roman victory was dampened by the outbreak of plague among the troops, which spread throughout the Empire.[5] Nevertheless the outcome was another major humiliation for Parthia. The Romans gained territory, including Dura Europos, and a third major setback was to follow.

From 193-197 Septimius Severus fought to establish his mastery of the Roman world. The emperor faced rivals in the East and in Britain. His eastern rival, Niger, received Parthian support. In retaliation for this, Severns advanced to Ctesiphon against minimal resistance and captured it early in 198. It was the third time Parthia's capital had fallen in less than a century. The Arch of Severus in

Rome depicts a battering ram striking the walls of Ctesiphon while a testudo ("tortoise" i.e. troops protected by shields in front and on top) advances on the enemy capital. Severus failed twice to take Hatra. By the time of Caracalla, however, Hatra had become an ally of Rome.

Severus' creation of two new provinces beyond the Euphrates, Osrhoene and Mesopotamia, constituted an even worse setback for Parthia than the spectacular but ephemeral gains of Trajan and Cassius. By annexing more territory Severus had advanced the frontiers of the Roman Empire closer to the Parthian heartland. Two new legions, I and III Parthica, were stationed at Singara and Nisibis, respectively.

Parthia fought well under its last king, Artabanus V, in its final conflict with the Romans under the emperor Macrinus. The battle of Nisibis in 217 was a Roman defeat, despite Roman skill in close combat, and a stratagem. Feigning a retreat, the Romans used caltrops, with their upwardly projecting spikes, to impale the pursuing horses and camels. Nevetheless, Parthian arrows and lances inflicted high losses on the legions. To secure peace, Macrinus had to pay a big indemnity and make unpopular concessions, dooming his reign in 218.

The achievement of Artabanus was rather modest, however, and the damage had been done. The disasters and humiliations of the second century had undermined confidence in the Parthian regime. By 218 it was probably too late to save it. The Iranians were ready to support a new dynasty which was to become a much more formidable enemy of Rome.

As early as the first century CE, native Persian culture was making a comeback in Iran. Parthia's kings were Hellenized, reflecting the increased Hellenization of the East in the wake of Alexander the Great. Native influences gradually reasserted themselves, contributing to the fall of Parthia.

Fars, in southern Iran, was the focus of the Persian revival. Sassan, high priest of the temple of Anahita at Persis, was succeeded by his son, Papak, who had greater ambitions. In 208 Papak overthrew a local prince and married his daughter. The Parthian king did not consider Papak or his son Shapur legitimate. Papak's second son, Ardashir, wished to replace Shapur as king of Persis, and did so when Shapur was assassinated.[6] Ardashir dominated Fars, Isfahan and Kerman, and compelled all the nobles of the area to recognize him. The Parthian king, Artabanus, ordered the king of Ahwaz to subdue Ardashir, but he failed. Ardashir then defeated the Parthian army in three battles. In the last battle, at Susiana in 224, Artabanus was killed. The head of the slain monarch was displayed in the temple of Anahita.

In 226 Ardashir was crowned king of a new Persian dynasty at Ctesiphon. This new dynasty, the "Sassanid," was named after Ardashir's grandfather, Sassan. The advent of Sassanid Persia was a watershed in the history of the Near East. For Rome, it augered a catastrophic era.

# The First Romano-Persian War, 229-233

The Sassanians probably did not seek to capture the entire area ruled by the old Achaeminid Empire. Nevertheless, Ardashir was quick to confront the Romans. In 229 or earlier he attacked Rome's ally Hatra. Not surprisingly, the attack failed. Hatra was a very strong citadel, resisting even Trajan and Severus. The Persians, however, undoubtedly learned from the failed assault of circa 228. Within a short time Sassanid troops were to become masters of siege warfare, succeeding where Rome failed.

Ardashir's invasion of Mesopotamia resulted in the defection of some Roman troops, who were attracted to the charismatic Persian. Other troops mutinied, killing Flavius Heracleo, the governor of Mesopotamia. Generally, legions I and III Parthica remained loyal, and crushed the mutinous troops. They could not, however, prevent the Persians from overrunning Mesopotamia.

Rome's emperor at the time, Alexander Severns, at first tried to negotiate with Ardashir. That attempt failed, and he brought many troops to the East.

The army of Alexander Severus was divided into three groups, with different objectives. The northernmost Roman force entered Armenia. Taking advantage of the rough terrain, which was ill suited to Persian cavalry, the Romans defeated the enemy, crossed the Tigris and invaded Media. The southern Roman force advanced along the Euphrates toward Ctesiphon, while the third force, with Alexander, acted as a reserve.

Ardashir launched his main counterattack against the southern force when it had advanced south of Dura Europos. According to the historian Herodian (or his source) the troops of the southern force advanced carelessly because they had met no resistance and assumed the Persians had been diverted away from them to deal with the other Roman forces. The central or reserve force of Alexander failed to support the southern force. Herodian based his account on a source hostile to the emperor, whom he considered a coward, dissuaded from risking his life by his mother. Alexander's failings supposedly led to the annihilation of the southern force. The Persians are said to have surrounded it and subjected the Romans to a hail of arrows. The trapped soldiers huddled together behind their shields and held out as long as possible. In the end, however, the Persians massacred the whole force; all the Romans are said to have been killed.

Herodian's source clearly attempted to portray Alexander Severns in the worst possible light. Exaggerating the extent of Roman losses was part of the slander. The claim that the southern column was wiped out is not credible. Alexander himself celebrated a triumph in September 233. In his report to the Senate, he claimed the capture of 30 of Persia's 700 war elephants and the killing of 200 others, plus 10,000 cataphracts killed and 200 chariots captured.[7] Moreover, a careful reading of Herodian's account reveals a number of inconsistencies:

—If all of the Romans of the southern column were killed, how did Herodian (or his source) know what they had thought beforehand e.g. about Persians being drawn elsewhere? Only survivors could have told them that.

—If all the Romans could do was try to protect themselves with their shields, how could the enemy have suffered many casualties in the battle, as indicated elsewhere in Herodian's account?

—Likewise, how could casualties have been equal on both sides if the southern column could not effectively resist, and was annihilated?

—If the Persian king had wiped out a Roman army, why didn't he exploit the success immediately with a renewed offensive, instead of disbanding his army? Ardashir did not resume attacking the Romans for years.

It seems most likely that the southern force, albeit mauled, fought the Persians to a draw. Among the Roman dead was the prefect of Legion IV Scythica. Although Alexander Severus' figures, above, are undoubtedly exaggerated, Persian losses were probably at least as severe as Roman losses. Ardashir's men were beaten in the north, and only achieved a bloody stalemate in the south. The Sassanids remained as determined as before, but they were still learning. In this first round they had not achieved tactical superiority over Roman forces, particularly the better legions or vexillations (detachments) from Europe. Nevertheless the Sassanids learned valuable lessons from the campaigns of 228-233, and gradually honed their military skills.

# Ardashir Strikes Again, 238-240

The Roman Empire was beset by civil war in 238. The emperor Maximinus I was slain, and ultimately Gordian III became emperor. The new emperor was only thirteen years old in 238.

Perceiving that Rome was temporarily distracted and weak, Ardashir quickly took advantage of the situation. A new Sassanian offensive began in 238, capturing Nisibis and Carrhae. The Persians attacked Dura Europos in 239, but the city resisted and held out. Ardashir's troops then assaulted Hatra, in 240, and finally succeeded in capturing it. Considering that Hatra had repelled all previous attacks, by Romans and Persians alike, and was bolstered by allied Roman troops by then, the Persian success is all the more remarkable. More than anything else, perhaps, the fall of Hatra attested to the growing prowess of the Sassanian army. It is most likely that Persian sappers undermined the walls of the citadel. The defenders of Dura Europos obviously anticipated this tactic several years later. They piled massive amounts of sand against their city wall to hold it upright. Elsewhere the walls of Roman cities fell to one side when undermined by sappers below, opening a breach which the Persian troops entered. This must have been the fate of Nisibis, Hatra and other strong points long before the Persians seriously attempted to take Dura Europos.

By the time of his death around 241, Ardashir had taken all of Roman Mesopotamia. His troops may have penetrated much farther, into Syria. The Antioch mint apparently ceased producing coins in 240-241, suggesting the Persians threatened or even took the city. The *Scriptores Historiae Augusta* states that Antioch was among the cities the Romans had to recapture, but it is not necessarily reliable. If Antioch was indeed taken, it was a further testament to the strength of the new Sassanid regime. Already in the time of Ardishir it had accomplished what the Parthians never did. The latter once besieged Antioch (circa 50 BCE,) but did not capture it.

The Roman counteroffensive was slow to develop because the Romans first had to deal with barbarian incursions in the Balkans. A great general, Timesitheus, became Praetorian Prefect and Gordian's father-in-law. He was the real power behind the puppet emperor. In 242 Timesitheus defeated the marauding Goths and Germans at Illyricum, and recruited some of them into the Roman army. In the third century, barbarian recruits were probably used to fill gaps in existing Roman units rather than form units of their own. There was an exception, however: a unit of barbarian horsemen. The Romans sought Gothic cavalry to oppose the powerful Persian cataphracts.

When logistical and other preparations were complete, the doors of the temple of Janus were opened, signifying a state of war with Persia. Gordian III and Timesitheus probably arrived in the East late in 242. By the following spring they were ready for war. Meanwhile, following Ardashir's death, his son Shapur became king of Persia. The father undoubtedly would have been proud had he lived to witness his son's reign. Rome's real time of troubles began with Shapur, albeit not right away.

# Shapur I Versus Gordian III 243-244

The Roman counterattack got underway in the spring of 243. Ably led by Timesitheus, the soldiers of II Traiana, II Parthica and other units drove the Persians out of Syria and Mesopotamia. Roman troops recaptured Carrhae, perhaps by storming the city. Sassanid forces retreated eastward with Timesitheus in pursuit. The Roman general probably won his greatest victory on the approaches to the Khabur near Rhesaina. Only one ancient source, Ammianus Marcellinus, mentioned Rhesaina, and we have no detailed account of the battle. Perhaps the Roman army bested Shapur's cavalry by luring it onto caltrops. After the horses were lamed, the legions surged forward, routing the Sassanids.[8] Persia's elite arm was not destroyed, but its losses were serious enough to compel a further major retreat. Moreover the weakened cavalry may have affected Sassanid performance in a later action, as will be seen.

The victors of Rhesaina did not emerge unscathed. Timesitheus may have perished in this battle. II Traiana recruited more men around this time, perhaps to replace battle casualties.

Rhesaina was almost the sole Roman victory over Shapur, but it was undoubtedly important. The Persians were forced to abandon Nisibis farther east, and Singara. Falling back past Dura Europos, the Sassanids lost all of Mesopotamia. Not even the death of Timesitheus halted the Roman offensive. His successor, Philip the Arab, continued it. After regaining Nisibis and Singara, the Romans turned back west, probably reaching the Khabur just north of Circesium. They marched along the east bank of the Khabur to Circesium, then along the east bank of the Euphrates toward Ctesiphon.[9] In a letter to the Senate, Gordian III made it clear that the Persian capital was the ultimate objective of the campaign, just as it had been in previous campaigns. Around February 244 the Roman army, advancing south of Dura Europos, encountered a Sassanian army at Meshike (or Misiche) blocking the way to Ctesiphon. The resulting clash marked the end of the young emperor, and of Roman ambitions in this war.

Meshike was undoubtedly a strategic victory for Persia, for the Romans did not reach Ctesiphon in 244. They withdrew, initially to the vicinity of Dura Europos. Gordian III was dead, and Philip, the new emperor, decided to buy peace with Persia, paying Shapur 500,000 denarii.

In the famous rock inscription at Naqs-i-Rustem, the *Res Gestae Divi Saporis* (RGDS) Shapur proclaimed a great victory. The emperor Gordian, he claimed, had sent an army drawn from the Goths and Germans as well as the whole Roman Empire, yet he had "annihilated" that force at Meshike and slain the emperor. Gordian III is depicted lying dead beneath Shapur's horse in the rock carving at Bishapur. At both Bishapur and Naqs-i-Rustem, Philip is shown kneeling before Shapur, as if pleading for peace after the disaster. The Persian king renamed Meshike Peros-Sabour, or "Victory of Shapur."

What happened at Meshike? How were the Romans stymied? There is no extant description of the battle. Fought in the same area as the confrontation of 233, Meshike was probably similar, with both sides taking heavy casualties. The following reconstruction seems most likely:

Gordian's men formed up for battle upon reaching the Persian army.[10] The Romans attacked, slowly pushing the enemy back in heavy fighting. With the legions fully engaged in front, the Persian cavalry moved against the Roman left flank. (The right flank of the southward-facing legions was presumably anchored on the east bank of the Euphrates.) The Gothic cavalry let the Romans down at this point. Acting as a flank guard, the Goths were crushed by Sassanid cataphracts, who then attempted to strike the Roman flank and rear. Gordian III personally led the Praetorian Guard into action to try to restore the situation. Adorned with regalia, and mounted on horseback, the young emperor was an inviting target for Persian archers or cataphract lances. In the course of fighting, Gordian was fatally struck by a projectile, just like Julian over a century later.

Seeing the grave threat posed by the Persian flanking attack, Philip and the legionary commanders ordered the troops to disengage from the frontal battle, and turn around to drive off the enemy. These men joined forces with the Praetorians to contain the enemy thrust, albeit at high cost. The cataphracts and bowmen withdrew, and the battle ended in a tactical draw.

The ability of the Romans to stave off complete disaster at Meshike may have owed much to their success at Rhesaina. If the Romans did maul the Sassanian cavalry then, the enemy elite may have been too weak to crush the legions in the subsequent engagement. There hadn't been enough time to train replacements in the interval between the two battles.

Shapur greatly exaggerated the magnitude of his victory. The Roman army was not wiped out in 244, not any more than it had been wiped out in 233. A gravestone in Turkey erected by a centurion of II Parthica in September 244 indicates the legion survived Meshike. Moreover, Roman troops built a monument or cenotaph for Gordian after the battle. The fact that Philip could spare soldiers for such a task suggests the Roman army was not severely depleted by Meshike, and nor was it seriously threatened by the Persians. It is noteworthy that Shapur agreed to accept money instead of trying to follow up the "annihilation" of the Roman army with a new offensive to regain Mesopotamia. The Romans may have been stopped, but the Persians were also bloodied. Shapur was nowhere near as successful in 244 as he would be in 252 and 260 when Roman armies were really destroyed.

It is significant that Gordian's remains were buried either at Zaitha near Circesium, or at Rome. His body did not fall into Persian hands.[11] That indicates the Romans had possession of the battlefield right after Meshike, implying a successful response to the crisis, save for the emperor's death. Again, the circumstances of Julian's death may parallel those of 244. History may have repeated itself. Meshike seems to have been far less of a tactical defeat than a strategic one. The Romans failed to reach Ctesiphon, but still performed well in battle.

After the disastrous setbacks of 243, the king of kings had to magnify his victory at Meshike to preserve his prestige, possibly even his regime. Hence the claim of total victory and the new name Peros Sabour. They were a reflection of political needs, not historical truth.

One lesson that Shapur apparently learned from the battles of 242-244 was that only the eastern Roman army could be easily overcome. Roman troops from Europe were more formidable, so the Sassanids apparently decided to wait for circumstances in which such troops could not reinforce the Roman East, before attacking it again.

Of all the ancient writings on this period, perhaps the most truthful and informative on the Roman side is a certain passage by Zosimus. He mentioned Gordian fighting the Persians and losing his life in the enemy's territory. Yet, he continued, even after that disaster the Persians were not able to take any part of the Roman Empire. The latter statement certainly appears true. In the next war the Persians had to capture Anatha and Dura Europos, the previous limits of the empire. Other than some possible concessions in Armenia, Rome did not cede any territory in 244. A passage by Zonaras mentioning an alleged counterattack by Philip to regain Armenia and Mesopotamia is not credible. Philip was eager for peace because he wished to go to Rome to consolidate his position as emperor. After Gordian's death the key issue was the succession.

The Roman authorities covered up the defeat at Meshike. It involved the first-ever death of an emperor in battle with a foreign enemy. A setback of that nature had to be concealed to preserve the morale of the empire in this difficult period. Philip originally claimed that Gordian had died of natural causes. Later, after Philip was overthrown and killed, his opponent, Decius, encouraged a new story. Gordian's demise was now blamed on Philip's alleged treachery.

Many ancient writers have echoed the official line that Roman troops murdered Gordian III at the instigation of Philip. Aurelius Victor, Festus, Eutropius, Jerome, Marcellinus, etc. all repeated this line. Philip is supposed to have diverted grain ships, causing the hungry troops to turn on Gordian. This oft-repeated story is simply not credible. Three ancient writers—Festus, Eutropius and Jerome—wrote that the Roman troops built a monument for Gordian III not far from Circesium. Ammianus Marcellinus reported seeing this monument (or "tomb") during Julian's fourth century expedition. It would have made no sense for the Roman troops to build a monument for Gordian if they had just turned against him and murdered him. The clear implication of the monument is that Gordian was held in high esteem by the soldiers to the end. They probably admired him for being a genuine commilitone (fellow soldier). Although many emperors addressed their troops as "fellow soldiers" it usually had a hollow ring. Emperors, being generally old, commanded but did not fight themselves. As a young man of about 18 in 244, Gordian III was an exception. A passage from Zonaras mentions him riding his horse into battle. The soldiers respected an emperor who was willing to risk his life alongside them. Indeed, if the reconstruction of Meshike, above, is correct, Gordian sacrificed his life to save theirs. His hypothesized quick action to stop an enemy flanking attack may have saved the whole army at the cost of his own life.

The fact that soldiers eager to return to their homes in Europe were willing to stay at Zaitha until the monument was finished says much about their gratitude to the fallen emperor. Nothing could be further from the truth than the official version.[12]

Despite the tendency to parrot official propaganda, five western historians appear to corroborate the Persian version of Gordian's death.[13] The passage from Zosimus, above, clearly implies Gordian was killed in battle, as it states he fought the Persians, and lost his life in their country. Zosimus' claim that the Persians were not able to take Roman territory despite the disaster is further confirmation. Why might the Persians be thought capable of exploiting the "disaster" i.e. Gordian's death, if they had not caused it as part of a victory over Rome? A mere usurption would not have weakened Rome vis a vis Persia, only a military setback, which in this case involved the emperor's death.

Why wasn't Zosimus (or his original source) more explicit? Why did they just imply death in battle, and not state it clearly? Undoubtedly the reason was official secrecy. As was noted above, concealing the truth was deemed essential for morale in a very trying period. Any writer who failed to adhere to the government line could have been arrested for sedition, and possibly executed. This did not prevent a few historians from at least hinting at the truth, however.

Malalas wrote that during a battle against Persian forces, Gordian was brought down from his steed, breaking his thigh. Monachos claimed he fell from his horse during a battle, resulting in a broken thigh and death. Cedrenus wrote almost the same thing, while Zonaras, after mentioning Gordian riding into battle to encourage his men, stated that he died after the horse stumbled and fell on him, causing a crushed thigh.

The story of falling from a horse, like the account of Zosimus, was the closest a late Roman historian could come to telling the truth without getting into trouble. It is a half truth, but clearly hints at the truth.

Struck by an enemy missile, Gordian toppled over with his horse. He may have broken his thigh, but that was not the primary cause of death. The young emperor died of hemorrhaging after all attempts to succor him failed. The Sassanids had scored another "first;" the killing of a Roman emperor.

Despite some achievements, the outcome for Shapur and the Sassanids in 244 was far from ideal. For the next several years they rebuilt and improved their forces while waiting for more favorable circumstances to resume war on Rome. They may have derived encouragement from the ouster of Priscus, whom Philip had entrusted to watch over the East while he set out for Rome.

Appointed Rector Orientis by Philip, Priscus probably had a mission similar to that of Corbulo and Avidius Cassius: improve the fighting quality of the eastern legions, largely by strengthening discipline. The imposition of stricter discipline probably made Priscus unpopular among the troops. Eventually they turned on him. Jotapianus, a would-be emperor, overthrew Priscus in 248. This coup did not bode well for the Romans. Any improvement effected by Priscus in the four years of his tenure was likely undone in the interval between his fall and the next eastern war. Without a strong authority such as Priscus, the eastern legions probably reverted to being slack, as had happened before. This contributed to the catastrophe which soon befell the Roman East.

248 witnessed another usurper, Pacatianus. Like Jotapianus, he aspired to the purple, but both were murdered. The next year

Decius more successfully challenged Philip, defeating and killing him at Verona.

For the time being the East remained quiet. Shapur evidently did not feel that conditions were ripe to attack anew until late 251. At last he received news which indicated he would not have to face Roman reinforcements. That he waited until this condition was met says much about the prowess of II Parthica, II Traiana, the Praetorians and other European Roman forces. They must have fought consistently well in the East, even at Meshike. Had Shapur been confident that he could deal with those troops on the basis of the experience of 244, he may have gone to war again before 250. By 252 he finally had a good reason to be confident.

# Shapur's Second Campaign, 252

Soon after he supplanted Philip as emperor, Decius had to return to the Balkans to battle invading Goths. During the course of this conflict the European legions were badly depleted. Cniva, leader of the Goths, destroyed much of Decius' army at Beroe Augusta Trajana in 250. About a year later, in July 251, Decius confronted the barbarians with a new army at Forum Terebronii or Abrittus. Cniva's Goths were drawn up in three lines, the rearmost behind a bog. The Romans defeated the first and second lines, and reached the bog. Decius then blundered by ordering his men into the morass to engage the third Gothic line behind it. Unable to fight effectively, the Roman army perished along with Decius and his son.[14]

Gallus, who succeeded Decius, inherited an empire which for the time being had been severely weakened. Abrittus had cost the Romans many of their best troops. Those that remained had to confront the continued menace of the victorious Goths. Rome also faced Franks and other barbarians. Few troops could be spared for the East should war break out there as well.

News of the Roman disaster presumably reached Shapur toward the end of 251. The Sassanians understood the opportunity Abrittus gave them, and wasted no time exploiting it. The *Res Gestae Diva Saporis* claims the Romans provoked the war by lying and harming Armenia. That was at best a pretext, if not an outright invention. In the spring of 252 the Persian army launched a major invasion northward along the Euphrates, capturing one Roman city after another. Anatha, an island city in the Euphrates, was the first to fall. Advancing past it, the Sassanids took Dura Europos, Circesium, Birtha and Sura. The Roman army of the east made its stand farther up the river at Barbalissos, east of Antioch.

Some historians have suggested that the Romans were planning a big offensive against Persia in 252, and that Shapur acted to preempt it, but that is ludicrous. The Roman Empire was clearly in no shape to undertake major offensive operations in the East in the aftermath of Abrittus. The theory of a planned offensive is based on two lines of evidence, neither of them strong: The increased output of antoniniani (coins used to pay soldiers) at the Antioch mint, and the arrival of vexillations from II Parthica at Apamaea in Syria.

The minting of more antoniniani is easily explained by the massing of a large army at Barbalissos. That was clearly a defensive deployment, since Barbalissos was far from Sassanid territory, and the Persians were advancing toward it. As for the detachments of II Parthica at Apamaea, that too was a defensive move, and far from adequate, as events were to prove.

Based in Italy, II Parthica was the only legion which still fought as a whole legion by the time of Gordian III's Persian war. All the other legions sent out vexillations. By the mid-third century, even II Parthica operated in vexillations. Whereas the whole legion presumably fought at Rhesaina and Meshike, with the rest of the emperor's strategic reserve, the Praetorian Guard, only a portion of the legion was in Syria in 252. Unlike Gordian III, Gallus was essentially a do-nothing emperor who did not go to the East with the reserves. He probably just sent a few vexillations to Syria in response to the governor's plea for reinforcements, as Shapur advanced. The European legions were still struggling to recuperate, so token assistance was all that Gallus could afford.

Defense of Syria now depended solely on the eastern army, which had repeatedly proven ineffective in the past, and was no deterrent to Sassanian aggression.

The battle of Barbalissos confirmed Shapur's low opinion of the Syrian legions. It was the greatest and most complete victory of his reign up till then, and the worst disaster to befall Roman arms in centuries. Shapur boasted that he wiped out 60,000 Roman troops at Barbalissos. The figure may well be accurate. The Sassanian army essentially eliminated the entire Roman army of the East in a single battle. The eastern legions may not have been 100% destroyed. The arrival of troops from IV Scythica at Dura Europos in 254 indicates that part of the legion survived. Not all of its men, or those of other units, were at Barbalissos. Some are thought to have garrisoned Syrian cities. There is no doubt, however, that the vast bulk of the eastern army was gone. There is no mention of any resistance by regular Roman troops to the subsequent Persian sack of Syria. Barbalissos left the whole province almost defenseless. Right after this victory the Persian army was split up into three plundering groups. One of these captured and looted Antioch, then Seleucia, Alexandria, Cyrrhos and Nicapolis. A second force plundered Zeugma, Doliche and Cappadocia, and the third sacked Apamaea, Raphanaea and Arethusa. The Persian army would not have been divided had there been any substantial Roman field army left in Syria after Barbalissos, or if any of the targeted cities had a large enough garrison to require a large Persian army to subdue. The clear implication is that the eastern army was practically wiped out. Only a local leader, Uranius Antoninus, effectively defended his city, Emesa, from Persian raiders. Given the appalling ineffectiveness of Rome's eastern force, it is not surprising that the Palmyrenes also relied more on their own forces in subsequent years.

How did the Persians destroy such a huge Roman force? We can only speculate, since there is no surviving description of Barbalissos. It is likely, however, that the Persians bypassed the Romans right flank. The left flank of the southward-facing army was presumably anchored on the Euphrates or the fortifications of Barbalissos itself. Cavalry could only get around the right flank to the west in the open desert. Sassanid horsemen quickly routed their Roman counterparts guarding the right flank, then fell upon the enemy infantry from the rear. Persian infantry, meanwhile, engaged the Romans frontally and held them in place. The result was a slaughter. Surrounded by the enemy, few Romans escaped, if any did.

Not surprisingly, the Romans covered up the disaster. Had it not been for the discovery of the RGDS in the 1930s, Barbalissos may never have been known to us. No Roman source mentioned it. The coverup was understandable. If all of the catastrophes of the period had become generally known, morale might've collapsed and western civilization with it.

The Roman authorities in Syria had blundered badly by making their stand at Barbalissos. It would've been much wiser to adopt a "medieval" approach i.e. move as much food and wealth as possible behind city walls or fortifications defended by all available forces. The main Sassanian asset, the cavalry, was not of much use against walled cities. In fact the Romans had effectively withstood the Parthian sieges of Antioch, circa 50 BCE. They presumably adopted this "medieval" approach in the aftermath of Carrhae, which demonstrated the difficulty of confronting the eastern enemy in open battle. By opting to fight the Persians in the field in 252, the Romans played right into their hands, with disastrous results. Their eastern territories were devastated.

After the shattering defeats of 251-252, many concluded that the Roman army could no longer provide adequate security. Diminished confidence in the army is reflected in the construction or strengthening of city walls throughout the East and in the rest of the Empire. The walls of Rome itself were refurbished and extended in the latter third century.

Shapur apparently understood that Roman weakness would not last indefinitely, and that his window of opportunity was limited. He anticipated that Roman reinforcements would eventually reach the East, just as they did in 242. Based on the experience of that war, the Sassanids had no intention of fighting those reinforcements. Rather than attempt to hold Syria and Mesopotamia, the Persians withdrew with their plunder. The emperor Valerian apparently regained the East with little difficulty in 254. His troops even retook Dura

Europos.[15] Sassanian caution reflected the lessons of the past, but the great successes of the second campaign emboldened Shapur in the next round.

# Shapur Versus Valerian, 256-260

Buoyed by the successes of 252, the Sassanians soon resumed hostilities, albeit on a limited scale at first. Around 256, Shapur's troops were fighting to regain Dura Europos.

Excavations at the site in the 1930s revealed the course of operations. As was noted previously, the Persians attempted to undermine the city walls by tunneling beneath them. The Romans dug a countermine to try to disrupt the Persian operations, but the effort failed. Persian troops entered the city and overcame the defenders manning the walls. Resistance ended at that point. Dura Europos suffered the same fate as Hatra. The city was abandoned and its citizens were deported.

The latest Roman coins found in Dura Europos date to 254, well before the fall of the city. The siege probably lasted into 257, or even began in that year. Even before the siege, the remote Dura garrison may not have received the latest minted coins.

Valerian's troops made no known attempt to relieve Dura Europos. Inaction may have resulted from the emperor's temporary absence from the East. He had to go to the West to help repel the Frankish invasions, which began in 256. Valerian and his son Gallienus (joint ruler in the West) were at Cologne in August 257. Not until the following spring did the father-emperor return to the East.

Inasmuch as the emergency in Gaul probably required the withdrawal of some eastern units, a relief of Dura was not possible. It would've provoked a full-scale war for which the Romans were not ready. Perhaps Shapur besieged Dura in 257 to take advantage of Roman weakness that year.

Since Valerian had returned to the East in 258, some have opined that the legendary defeat and capture of the emperor occurred then, or in 259, as Lopuszanski concluded. This is dubious. Coins and papyri found in Egypt indicate Valerian was still considered the emperor in August 260. Communications were not so slow that news of his elimination would have failed to reach Egypt for 1-2 years. Loss of an emperor probably would've been reflected in official documents and coinage in just a few months, especially since Egypt is rather close to Syria.

Surprisingly, Maurice Sartre accepted Lopuszanski's view that Valerian was captured in 259 even though he wrote elsewhere that Antioch was sacked in 260. It wouldn't have taken the Persians a year to reach Antioch after besting Valerian at nearby Edessa.[16]

Beset by Gothic seaborne raiders, plague and other troubles, Valerian sought help in looking after the East. In 258 he made

Odenathus Vir Consularius, foreshadowing a greater role for the Palmyrene after Valerian himself was gone. By conferring the title upon Odenathus, Valerian sought to retain his loyalty after the fall of Dura, not far from Palmyra. The timing suggests that Dura had fallen just the year before, 257, and another confrontation was looming.

After the Dura campaign, Shapur probably spent the next two years building up his army and honing its skills. He now felt confident his troops could overcome the cream of the Roman army, providing they could again fight it in an open battle. The Persian commanders devised a strategy to lure Valerian onto terrain favorable for cavalry warfare, in which the Persians excelled.

In the spring of 260 the Sassanians again advanced in force against the Roman Empire. Shapur's army may have proceeded along the east bank of the Khabur from Circesium to Rhesaina, then turned westward to Edessa and Carrhae, which they besieged. Edessa itself was apparently of no interest to the Persians. They did not capture that city, probably because that was not their real intention.

The least valuable Persian troops, the paighan or peasant infantry, were often used in siege operations. These troops presumably surrounded Edessa and Carrhae while the cataphracts and other elite units were held in reserve. Because the fighting quality of the paighan was low, the Romans, it was hoped, would be tempted to strike at them and relieve the cities. That, of course, would enable the crack Sassanians to spring their trap. Sure enough, the Romans fell for the bait.

Generally, the ancient western record of these events is poor. The best version is one by Zonaras, who based it on the lost writings of Petrus Patricius. According to this account, Shapur's troops besieged Edessa, and Valerian at first hesitated to come and fight. Soon he was encouraged by the exploits of the Edessa garrison, who killed many of the besiegers. Valerian's army came and was surrounded by the enemy. Many soldiers were lost, some fled, and the emperor and his retinue were captured and taken to Shapur.

That scenario is very credible and consistent with the RGDS. The Nags-i-Rustem inscription mentions the siege of Edessa and Carrhae, the defeat of a 70,000-man Roman army and the capture of Valerian. After Barbalissos, only eight years before, Valerian no doubt had a healthy respect for the army of Shapur. But the poor quality of the paighan besiegers, revealed by the successes of Edessa's troops, emboldened the emperor. He led his army into terrain where it was easily surrounded. Bombarded with arrows, and assaulted by charging cataphracts, the army was destroyed, save for those who escaped.

It is possible that the siege of Dura Europos was Shapur's first attempt to lure the Romans into a trap. When it became clear, by 257-258, that the Roman army would not attempt to save Dura or retake it, Shapur may have decided that he had to be more provocative, besieging cities closer to Antioch.

Roman propagandists could not deny that Valerian had been captured. The Persians obviously had him, so they invented stories that he had been captured by treachery while attempting negotiations, or was taken while fleeing mutinous troops. None of these tales are credible. Even if Valerian' s army had become mutinous, he would have fled *west*, toward Gallienus, not east into captivity. As for the claim of treachery, it is noteworthy that Valerian's entire staff, or entourage, vanished with him. The RGDS claims the capture of the Praetorian prefect, army commanders, senators and others. That appears true, for there is no subsequent mention of Succesianus, the Praetorian prefect under Valerian. He presumably disappeared into captivity with his emperor. The capture of so many Romans of high rank could only have resulted from a major military defeat. Even if Valerian did try to negotiate, it is doubtful that all those high officials would've accompanied him. Who would look after the army and government if something went wrong?

Gallienus was almost certainly behind the mutiny and trickery stories. By blaming wily Persians or mutinous Romans, he sought to make it appear that Valerian was taken through no fault of his own. Understandably, Gallienus tried to mitigate his father's disgrace. The capture of an emperor by a foreign enemy was probably the most humiliating episode in Roman history. It was the nadir of the catastrophic era.

Even worse than the loss of Valerian was the destruction of his army, part of which was never rebuilt. There is no record of Legion VI Ferrata after 260. Some of its men may have carved the reliefs at Naqs-i-Rustem and Bishapur commemorating their defeat.

For Shapur, Edessa was the climax of his reign. He had become the greatest nemesis of Rome since Hannibal. Barbalissos and Edessa were among the greatest battles of antiquity. For Rome, they were defeats of an enormity rivaling Cannae.

There have been conflicting views concerning the fate of Valerian. Western writers, notably the Christian Lactantius, have tended to depict a terrible fate. Shapur supposedly used Valerian as a footstool, and stepped on the emperor's back when he mounted his horse. Ultimately, Lactantius claimed, Valerian was stuffed as a trophy in a Persian temple. Such tales have been widely believed, along with other lies about this period.[17] Edward Gibbon, however, rightly doubted them. He noted that a monarch such as Shapur would not have defiled the majesty of another king, even if he were a rival. To do so would set a bad example, potentially undermining his own status.

The claim that Shapur routinely stepped on Valerian's back is ludicrous. The emperor was an aged man of 60 when captured. He couldn't have borne the full weight of another man on his back or shoulders. It would've killed or crippled him the first time.

Roman propagandists may have invented these stories to whip up hatred of Persia during the subsequent campaigns of Carus and Galerius. The Christians clearly wanted to believe that Valerian, a persecutor, had reached a terrible end, and so favored this version. Inasmuch as the Christians eventually took over the West, it is not surprising that it prevailed for so long.

Western horror stories about Valerian contrast greatly with the account of Firdawsi, a Persian epic poet. Firdawsi wrote that Shapur took Valerian with him, and listened to him speak on various matters. Many captured Romans were put to work building a bridge over the Karun river. Part of this bridge is still extant, confirming the poet's account.[18] There is absolutely no corroboration of the western stories in Persian sources. Valerian lived under fairly good conditions in Bishapur, where the famous rock reliefs tend to refute the horrid tales. The emperor is depicted in full regalia, being held by the mounted Shapur. Although a captive, he is neither chained nor prostrate.

Shapur's men plundered the Roman East after Edessa, just as they had done after Barbalissos. Before the looting commenced, however, there was a military mopping-up operation. The RGDS suggests that Samosata was the Persian army's first objective after Edessa. Macrianus, prefect of the annona, or military supplies, apparently had some reserve troops at Samosata. Injured in the foot, the prefect had been unable to fight at Edessa. Nor could he, a cripple, seek the purple for himself after the loss of Valerian. Shapur sent Cledonius, a captured Roman official, to Macrianus to ask him to come to Valerian, or in essence to surrender. Macrianus refused. The Sassanids then struck at Samosata, capturing it, but Macrianus retained enough strength to proclaim his two sons emperors.

After taking Samosata, the Persians sacked Antioch and about thirty other cities. They took some civilians captive. The raiders encountered greater resistance this time, however. A Roman general, Callistus (nicknamed "Ballista") took command of the stragglers from Edessa. Rallying these men, he counterattacked in Lykaonia, killing 3,000 Persians. The Sassanids by then were too dispersed while looting to fight effectively. Alarmed by the counterattack, Shapur withdrew. He bribed the able garrison at Edessa to let him pass undisturbed. Odenathus, however, harassed Shapur's retreating columns, and reached Ctesiphon once or twice around 262. The Palmyrene forces inflicted only moderate damage, however, and did not capture the Sassanian capital.

Notwithstanding his successes in battle, Shapur did not attempt to permanently occupy Syria. The region could not be held for long even if Persian forces were a match for the emperor's. Unlike the standing Roman army, the Sassanid forces were disbanded after a campaign. They could not defend remote areas against a counterattack which could come at any time. Rather than try to annex Syria, Shapur transferred as much of its wealth and talent as possible to Persia.

# Palmyra and Aurelian

Odenathus was initially a great asset to Gallienus. Even in its darkest hour, Rome still inspired confidence and loyalty. There would be no lasting Persian domination of the East. A letter from the king of Armenia warning Shapur of Roman resiliency is another propaganda invention, but it still reflected the views of many. The Palmyrene leader served Gallienus well, striking at usurpers in the East as well as Shapur. Macrianus' sons were recognized as emperors in Egypt by late 260, as a papyrus indicates, but they were soon eliminated. One lost his life with his father at Serdica in 261. Odenathus eliminated the other son, Quietus, who had remained in the East, and Callistus, another would-be emperor.

With the usurpers out of the way, Odenathus launched an offensive against the Persians in 262. As was noted, above, the Palmyrene troops reached Ctesiphon, perhaps twice.[19] It is likely that the initiative for this operation came from Gallienus. He was eager to avenge the defeat of his father and force the

Persians to return him. The offensive, however, was not effective enough.[20]

Considering the magnitude of Shapur' s victory at Edessa, it is surprising how supine he appeared afterwards. There is no evidence of a Persian counterattack against Odenathus in response to the latter's assaults of 260, 262 and perhaps later. Odenathus may have besieged Shapur in Ctesiphon, but suffered no known retribution. Perhaps the Persian king, now aging, was content to rest on his laurels and enjoy the spoils of his victories.

Gallienus eventually felt that Odenathus had become too powerful and independent. Romans probably instigated the assassination of the Palmyrene around 267. The result, however, was a worse challenge to Imperial authority.

Zenobia, the widow of Odenathus, and her son Vaballathus, sought to become the new masters of the Roman world. By September 270, with up to 70,000 troops, Zenobia had taken over Syria, Palestine, much of Asia Minor and Egypt.

Proclaimed emperor in 270, Aurelian was determined to regain the East. He launched his campaign in 272, defeating the Palmyrenes at Tyana and Immae, near Antioch, then at Emesa. The latter victory was decisive. Palmyra fell in August 272. Soon afterwards, Zenobia was captured. The crushing of a new Palmyrene rebel, Apsaios, marked the end of resistance.

The battle of Emesa did more than restore the Roman Empire in the East. It restored confidence in Roman armies. Shapur's great victories led many to believe that Roman forces, composed of infantry, were obsolete. Cavalry, it seemed, now dominated the battlefield. The widespread perception that Roman armies had been eclipsed led Palmyrenes and others to build their own forces.

Emesa changed that. Palmyrene cavalry chased away the mounted Roman flank guards, but the infantry wheeled their ranks around to face the cataphracts to the rear. The Romans then attacked the enemy, now scattered in pursuit. The result was a great victory of Roman infantry over cataphracts.

The training of Aurelian's legions presumably reflected the lessons of Barbalissos and Edessa, and thus may shed light on those battles. Drilling the new Roman army of 272 to efficiently turn around suggests that Shapur's cavalry did indeed strike the Romans from behind in 252 and 260. That tactic was presumably what Roman training was intended to counter.

The Roman deployment at Maranga in 363 may also shed light on the great disasters of 252 and 260. Julian's army employed a crescent formation to prevent encirclement and repel flank attacks.

Rectifying the weakness and indiscipline of the third century army enabled Aurelian to become the "restorer of the world." While Rome was in the ascendant, its eastern enemy was in decline.

For some reason the Persian threat, so formidable from 230-260, seems to have evaporated for most of the latter third century. There is no evidence that Palmyra sought Persian help to repel Aurelian. Perhaps it just wasn't available. Shapur died that same year, 272. Without effective leadership the Sassanids could not intervene.

Persian power, like Parthian power, fluctuated remarkably over time. Beset by internal troubles (or other enemies) the victors of Carrhae could offer scant resistance to Severns' march to Ctesiphon. They went from dominance to near-impotence. The Sassanians had come to power to rectify this weakness, but were subject to the same pathologies. After attaining their peak: around 260 the Sassanians seemed to fade away for years.

# The Later Restorers

Power struggles contributed greatly to Sassanid weakness. Varham II, the Persian king 276-293 CE, ceded Armenia and Mesopotamia to the Romans in order to deal with his brother, who sought the throne. Rome, meanwhile, was again in capable hands.

By the time of Aurelian, the Illyrians had taken over the Roman Empire. Inasmuch as Illyricum had been a major source of troops for a century it is not surprising that its men ultimately dominated the Empire. The army was the most important source of an emperor's support. Eventually the Illyrian troops demanded that one of their own be emperor. The rapid succession of emperors did not cease, but by the latter third century one Illyrian succeeded another.

The Illyrians were the backbone of the late Roman world. They were the principal (if not the only) group which was still prepared to take on the mantle of the original Romans. For some reason, probably centuries of soldiering, the Illyrians had internalized

Roman ways and continued them even in the face of new and competing influences such as Christianity. They were still willing to do the hard fighting necessary to preserve the Empire. Indeed, it is tempting to conclude that the fall of the Western Empire was due to the division of the Empire into eastern and western halves in 395. Essentially, the division meant that the Illyrians, who resided in the East, no longer had any responsibility for the West. Bereft of Illyrian support, the Western Empire soon crumbled away. With few exceptions, its own citizens were nowhere near as dedicated or motivated.[21] By contrast, the Eastern Empire lasted another millennium.

Illyrian strength, coupled with Persian weakness, enabled the emperor Carus, in 283, to replicate the feat of Trajan. Less than a quarter century after Shapur's greatest victory, the Romans captured Ctesiphon, virtually without resistance. It was a remarkable comeback for an empire which only a generation before had seemed all but destroyed.

The Sassanians did campaign effectively, at first, during the reign of Diocletian (284-305). The new Persian king, Narses, invaded Armenia. When Diocletian's collegue, Galerius, tried to intervene, Narses smashed his army near Carrhae in 296. Carrhae II is yet another third century battle for which we have no detailed account. It may have represented another failure of the eastern legions. The Roman defeat was probably due to the Persian cavalry taking advantage of favorable terrain. In the next round, Galerius battled the Sassanids in Armenia, where rugged terrain was less favorable to Persia's elite arm.

The Romans avenged their defeat in 298. With 25,000 troops, Galerius assaulted the Persian camp and massacred the army of

Narses, who fled, wounded. The victors seized the Persian treasury and royal harem. Beaten decisively, Narses was forced to concede everything.[22] The treaty of 299 saw all of the disputed territory, including Armenia and Media, pass into Roman hands. The Romans consolidated their gains with a new defense system, the Strata Diocletiana, which stymied Persia for many years.

The Roman comeback was complete. The Empire had withstood a catastrophic era comparable to the Second Punic War, when Hannibal inflicted a series of massive defeats. Remarkably, the Roman Empire of the East circa 300 was larger and stronger than it had been in the time of the Severi, before the catastrophes struck. Rome's amazing resiliency, which overcame Hannibal, now undid the ravages of Shapur. Inherited by the Illyrians, this resilient spirit did not last much longer in the West.[23]

# End Notes

1. Conflict erupted during Nero's reign over the succession to the Armenian throne. Rome used Armenia as a buffer between Parthia and its eastern territories, and required a pro-Roman king in Armenia for this.
2. Parthia did not intervene during the Jewish revolts of the first and second centuries. The first revolt began in 66 CE, and essentially ended in 70, when the Romans recaptured Jerusalem. The rebels held Masada for a few years afterwards, but it fell in 74. The second revolt broke out in 132. Led by Simon bar Kochba, the rebels apparently destroyed a Roman legion, Deotariana, but were finally beaten late in 135. They may never have captured Jerusalem, renamed Aelia Capitolina by the Romans.
3. Many were said to lack helmets.
4. Dura was itself besieged and taken.
5. Surprisingly, the plague did not prevent Cassius from launching another offensive, into Media, in 166. Presumably this success

occurred after some Roman troops contracted the plague at Seleucia near Ctesiphon.

6. Shapur's death was supposedly accidental, but this seems less likely than assassination.

7. Evidently, war elephants were not a new and fearsome element during Julian's campaign of 363, as Ferrill wrote. Alexander Severus clearly indicated that the Romans encountered them in 233. It is likely that the Sassanids used elephants at other times in the third century.

8. There is an interesting illustration of this scenario in *Imperial Roman Legionary 161-284.*

9. Millar suggested essentially the same route in *The Roman Near East.*

10. This army may have consisted mainly of peasant infantry, hastily mobilized in the emergency after Rhesaina. High quality Dailamite infantry may also have been present at Meshike.

11. The relevant passage from the RGDS has been rendered as "...Gordian was destroyed..." The Persians did not have the body of Gordian to verify his death in battle. Witnesses among their cavalry probably claimed he was hit and fell.

12. Dodgeon and Lieu seemed reluctant to believe Gordian was killed in battle. They wrote that Gordian's cenotaph was located in Persian territory, at Zaitha. In fact, the area remained under Roman control after 244. The location of the cenotaph at Zaitha does not argue against Gordian being killed at Meshike. The Romans could not build a cenotaph at Meshike because that was in Persian territory. They had to abandon the invasion of enemy territory and pull back to their own, before building a cenotaph. Dodgeon and Lieu noted that Philip did not suffer damnatio memoriae. The fact

that Philip's accusers did not take their charge seriously enough to erase his memory argues that he was not responsible for Gordian's death. Therefore, they suggested, Gordian was killed by Roman troops acting on their own initiative. While it is certainly true that Philip was blameless, the troops weren't responsible either. Again, the cenotaph indicates they had not turned against Gordian.

13. The tradition of blaming Philip has persisted until quite recently. See e.g. Grant *The Roman Emperors*. Kettenhofen and Hartman, however, came to a different conclusion, while Sartre, in *The Middle East Under Rome*, rightly rejects the tradition. The Romans often blamed setbacks on the alleged treachery of those who fell out of favor afterwards. Gallus was blamed for the defeat at Abrittus. The naval defeat of 468 was attributed to the treachery of Basiliscus after his ouster in 476. Other examples can be cited.

14. Abrittus is in the vicinity of modern Razgrad, Bulgaria. Evidently, archeologists have not found the site of the battle. It is possible that the bog preserved many Roman soldiers, complete with armor. If such remains are ever found they could shed much light on how Roman soldiers of the period were armed. By the third century, lorica segmentata, well known from Trajan's Column, was being phased out in favor of mail and scale armor. Likewise, the Imperial Gallic helmets of the high Empire were replaced by spangenhelm and Romano-Sassanian helmets. It would be interesting to know to what extent these changes had occurred by the time of Forum Terebronii (251). Perhaps the enormous losses in equipment incurred around mid-century compelled the switch to spangenhelm and Romano Sassanian helmets. As the latter types were cheaper and easier to produce, the Roman authorities may have opted for them at a time when many replacements were

needed quickly, yet money was limited. The transition to less costly head protection may have been due entirely to financial considerations. One of the Dura Europos frescoes, dated circa 244-246 i.e. before the worst of the mid century defeats, depicts soldiers wearing a coif or armored hood. The coif was less expensive than a helmet and may have been in widespread use by the time of Gordian III's Persian War. The Dura artist could have based the depiction on Roman troops marching past on their way to Ctesiphon or Meshike at the beginning of 244. Front rankers of II Traiana are shown with coifs in the Rhesaina painting in the book on Roman legionnaires.

15. The discovery of a document concerning the divorce of a soldier from IV Scythica indicates that troops from the legion were in Dura Europos in April 254. The separation of the soldier from his Dura wife during the initial Persian occupation of 252-254 probably caused both to find alternate partners. As this would've swiftly led to divorce, April 254 may well be the month Dura was reoccupied by the Romans.

While retaking the East, Valerian's troops eliminated Cyriades or Mariades, who had allegedly turned over Antioch to the Persians in 252, or who had been installed by Shapur as a puppet ruler. Shapur's withdrawal left Cyriades without support and he may have been burned alive by Valerian's troops at the end of 253.

16. Archeologists have not located the site of this battle, or the others mentioned. The present-day site of Meshike is at or near Fallujah, in al-Anbar province, Iraq. Present conditions are not conducive to research.

17. Surprisingly, Heather repeats the dubious tale of Valerian's humiliation in his *The Fall of the Roman Empire*. His claim that the

kneeling figure in the rock reliefs is Valerian is outdated. Moreover, contrary to his assertion, the figure is clearly not chained.
18. The account of al-Tabari, an Arab historian, is similar.
19. Heather portrays Persia as a "superpower rival" of Rome, compelling more taxation and larger armies to cope with. Actually, Persia seemed moribund for much of the latter third century.

Lactantius claimed that the Romans did not even demand the return of Valerian. Most historians have opined that Gallienus was unable to do anything to retrieve his father. It is likely, however, that Gallienus urged Odenathus to march to Ctesiphon as soon as possible, in 262, and that the offensive was intended in part to free Valerian or compel his return. At that time Valerian was not in Ctesiphon, but at Bishapur farther away. His whereabouts, however, may not have been known to Gallienus or Odenathus. They may have assumed the emperor was held captive with Shapur in the Persian capital. Or perhaps by taking Ctesiphon they could compel the Sassanids to return Valerian, wherever he was. Gallienus may have been motivated by considerations other than merely wishing to rescue his father. If Valerian could be retrieved and returned to power, that might have restored desperately needed stability to the Empire. Valerian was able to maintain discipline in the army and keep would-be usurpers at bay. He may not have been a great military commander, but he was still potentially an asset. It is clear that Odenathus faithfully served Gallienus by eliminating the would-be usurpers of 260-261. The advance to Ctesiphon was also clearly intended to serve Roman interests. It helped diminish Persian prestige after Edessa. Since Odenathus was obviously serving Gallienus, it is reasonable to assume the emperor in the West was behind the assault on Shapur's capital. He presumably wanted revenge, and his father back. As was noted previously, Gallienus was most likely the originator of stories that absolved Valerian of the responsibility for his capture. Doing whatever he could for his father was clearly on Gallienus' agenda. Apparently he did his best, albeit with allied troops, to rescue the old man. Conceivably, Gallienus ordered the elimination of Odenathus because he failed to take Ctesiphon again in 267.

By the fourth century, some men cut off their thumbs in an attempt to avoid military service.

22. Narses was grateful for the safe return of his wife and daughter. Galerius is said to have contrasted that with the supposed terrible fate of Valerian.

23. Heather blamed the fall of the Roman Empire on external enemies which became more effective in response to it. That included barbarians as well as Persians. This view is fallacious. The basic problem by the fifth century was lack of motivation within the Western Empire. Rome had long faced enemies which became more formidable in response to its power. Hannibal's army was an excellent example. The difference between the Hannibalic period and the fifth century was that the Romans were motivated during the former, but not the latter. Relatively few Roman citizens were willing to serve in the western army by the fifth century.

Printed in the United States
68833LVS00004B/41